The Baseball King

by Max C. Weiss

with illustrations by Linda Kay

Castadream Press

ISBN: 978-0-692-47520-1

About the Author

Max C. Weiss is an eight-year-old boy from New England. He is an avid baseball player and fan. He hopes to play for the Boston Red Sox when he grows up.

Acknowledgements

I'd like to thank my mom and dad for helping to make my story into a book. I'd like to thank Grandma Linda for the awesome illustrations. I'd like to thank Aunt Tiffy for the editing and fixing my mistakes.

To Annie, my little sister.

There once was a boy named Ryan.
He was ten years old.
He loved baseball.

Ryan played baseball every day after school

And he played all day on the weekends.

Ryan went outside to practice hitting the ball.
He hit the ball over and over and over.

Then his friend Max came by.

Max said, "Want to play a baseball game?"

Ryan happily said, "Yes!"

Ryan chose the Red Sox.

Max chose the Yankees.

"Play ball!" shouted Max, and the game started.

They played
    and played
        and played.

The final score was 5 to 7.

"Time to go to your game!" shouted Ryan's dad, Jaco.

Ryan then said to Max, "Thanks for the warm-up."

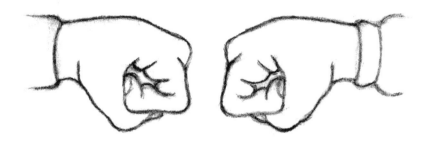

Ryan got in the car and left.

When Ryan got to his game he ran over to his coach, Jaydon, and asked, "When am I batting?"

"Third. You are also the starting pitcher," said the coach.

Coach Jaydon then said, "The game starts in ten minutes. Now go practice with your team."

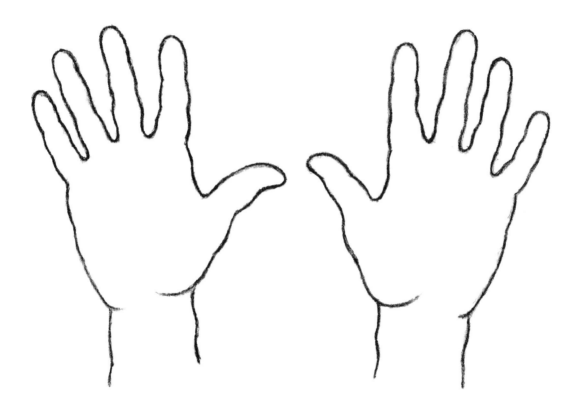

Ten minutes later the game started.

Over the next two hours,
Ryan had pitched many
wild balls and walked
many batters.

He also struck out twice.

Ryan was disappointed in the loss and with himself,
but he decided he wouldn't give up.

He would practice baseball whenever he could. Max often helped him.

Ryan swung the bat while his friends swung on the swings.

And he watched baseball while his friends watched cartoons.

And he caught baseballs while his friends caught sunrays on the beach.

And he threw baseballs while his friends threw parties.

And over and over, he practiced.

And he trained.

And he pushed his limits.

And while he worked very hard, he loved what he was doing, and he had fun.

Twelve years later …

Ryan stood tall
and confident
at the plate.

Max was the catcher
behind home plate.

World Series.

Bases loaded.

Two outs. Full count …
    … bottom of the ninth.

A home run to win the World Series!
Everyone went crazy!

Max took off his catcher's mask.
He gave Ryan a thumbs up and a smile.

And that's how Ryan became the baseball king.

The End

CPSIA information can be obtained at www.ICGtesting.com
Printed in the USA
BVOW07*0845160715

408214BV00001B/1/P